The
Tiara
Club

For dearest Charlotte,
always and for ever a princess,
with much love. xx
VF

For my big sis
Princess Charlotte.
SG

www.tiaraclub.co.uk

ORCHARD BOOKS
338 Euston Road, London NW1 3BH
Orchard Books Australia
Hachette Children's Books
Level 17/207 Kent Street, Sydney, NSW 2000
A Paperback Original
First published in Great Britain in 2005
Text © Vivian French 2005
Illustrations © Sarah Gibb 2005
The rights of Vivian French and Sarah Gibb to be
identified as the author and illustrator of this work
have been asserted by them in accordance with
the Copyright, Designs and Patents Act, 1988.

A CIP catalogue record for this book is available
from the British Library
ISBN 978 1 84362 863 7
10

Printed in Great Britain

The Tiara Club

Princess Charlotte
and the **Birthday Ball**

By Vivian French
Illustrated by Sarah Gibb

ORCHARD BOOKS

The Royal Palace Academy
for the Preparation of Perfect Princesses

(Known to our students as 'The Princess Academy')

OUR SCHOOL MOTTO:

*A Perfect Princess always thinks of others before herself,
and is kind, caring and truthful.*

We offer the complete curriculum for all princesses, including –

*How to talk
to a Dragon*

*Designing and Creating
the Perfect Ball Gown*

*Creative Cooking for
Perfect Palace Parties*

*Avoiding Magical
Mistakes*

*Wishes, and how
to use them Wisely*

*Descending a Staircase
as if Floating on Air*

Our head teacher, Queen Gloriana, is present at all times, and students are well looked after by the school Fairy Godmother.

Visiting tutors and experts include –

KING PERCIVAL
(Dragons)

QUEEN MOTHER MATILDA
(Etiquette, Posture and Poise)

LADY VICTORIA
(Banquets)

THE GRAND HIGH DUCHESS
DELIA (Costume)

We award tiara points to encourage
our princesses towards the next level.
All princesses who win enough points in their
first year are welcomed to the Tiara Club
and presented with a silver tiara.

Tiara Club princesses are invited to return
next year to Silver Towers, our very special
residence for Perfect Princesses, where
they may continue their education
at a higher level.

PLEASE NOTE:
Princesses are expected to arrive at the Academy
with a *minimum* of:

TWENTY BALL GOWNS
(with all necessary hoops,
petticoats, etc)

TWELVE DAY DRESSES

SEVEN GOWNS
suitable for garden parties,
and other special
day occasions

TWELVE TIARAS

DANCING SHOES
five pairs

VELVET SLIPPERS
three pairs

RIDING BOOTS
two pairs

Cloaks, muffs, stoles, gloves
and other essential
accessories as required

Hi! I'm Charlotte. Princess Charlotte. I'm VERY pleased to meet you, and I'm SO glad you're going to keep me company at the Princess Academy. It's a very special school for special princesses, and I don't know HOW Princess Perfecta or Princess Floreen got in! But you? You're EXACTLY right! So – WELCOME TO THE ACADEMY!

I've been wondering if you've ever had one of those days when absolutely EVERYTHING goes wrong? You have? Well, my very first day at the Princess Academy was just like that...

Chapter One

I stood in the doorway, and stared. I'd never seen a school dormitory before, and I couldn't believe my eyes. It was a long thin room, and although the walls were a lovely rose pink, it was so empty. Just six cupboards, six chairs, and six beds arranged in neat and tidy rows.

And a thought hit me – ZONK!!!!

I was going to have to SHARE with five other princesses!!

I gasped. I did my best to pretend it was a sort of cough, but it wasn't easy. And then I saw something else, and my mouth dropped open, and I totally couldn't close it.

NOT ONE of the beds had satin sheets! They were plain white cotton. They did look very sparkly clean, but all the same...how could ANY princess be expected to sleep on plain cotton sheets?

"Now dear, unpack your things, and make yourself at home." Queen Gloriana smiled at me as if everything was perfectly normal, and waved me towards the bed by the window.

"You're the first here in Rose Room, but the other princesses will be arriving any minute. They're all lovely girls, and I'm sure you'll be GREAT friends!" My new headmistress waved again as she swept away, her long velvet skirts brushing the floor as she went.

"Thank you, your majesty," I said as politely as I could, but my heart was thumping.

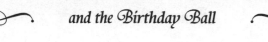

I hurried to the window, and looked out...and I was just in time to see my father's golden coach glinting in the sunshine before it turned the corner of the drive and disappeared.

If I hadn't heard someone coming up the stairs I'd have howled my eyes out. I mean, what WAS this place?

I'd been reading up about "The Royal Palace Academy for the Preparation of Perfect Princesses" for AGES. The brochure was full of pictures of sweeping staircases, and a magical lake with swans floating on their own reflections. Best of all, there was the Princess Academy Annual Birthday Ball. It looked FABULOUS. Imagine the most wonderful ballroom ever, with a dark blue ceiling lit by millions of tiny sparkly stars, and lots and lots of the most beautiful princesses in lovely LOVELY dresses twirling round and round the floor. And it all happened on the very first evening of the new school year!!!

I'd been dreaming about the Birthday Ball. I could SO imagine every head turning as I drifted onto the dance floor.

I'd decided that my dress would be soft pink with lots of swirly petticoats, and my tiara would be so sparkly that everyone would be completely dazzled. No one would EVER notice my hair was a little bit mousy, and my nose wasn't exactly perfect, because if I was at the Princess Academy Birthday Ball then I'd be beautiful too.

I nagged and NAGGED Mum and Dad until they said I could go to the Academy, and then I nagged a whole lot more until Mum agreed to let me have the dress I'd imagined.

(It wasn't EXACTLY right, but it was very nearly.) I counted every single day until the beginning of term...

...but as I stared miserably out of the window I knew I'd made a HUGE mistake. Queen Gloriana was scary. The school was too big. The dormitory was horrid. I didn't want to share a room with anyone, let alone five girls I'd never ever met.

I decided I absolutely HAD to run away. At once.

"Hello," said a voice from the doorway, and I turned, blinking hard so whoever it was wouldn't see I was nearly crying.

Chapter Two

You know how sometimes you see someone, and you just KNOW you're going to be best friends? Well, it was like that when I saw Princess Alice. She's got SUCH pretty pink cheeks, and dark hair that sort of bubbles around her face, and the loveliest smile.

She was smiling as she came bouncing into the room.

"It's a bit grim, isn't it?" she said cheerfully. "My big sister was here last year, and she told me it was like prison! It's supposed to be good for us, and make us grateful for what we've got at home."

She flung her suitcase on the bed next to mine. "Do you mind?" she asked. "Only I don't want to be next to someone I don't like."

I felt a sort of glow inside. "That's fine by me," I said.

Alice grinned. "Let's hope the

others are OK. My sis was next to a princess who was SO untidy the whole dormitory was ALWAYS getting minus tiara points! And she snored!"

I couldn't help giggling, but I didn't know what she meant. "What are tiara points?"

"It's brilliant!" Alice's eyes sparkled. "When you get five hundred – if you ever do – you get to join the Tiara Club!" She sighed ecstatically. "I can't WAIT! There's a fantastically wonderful party to celebrate, and you're given a whole LOAD of presents, and you get to go up to the second year! And then you're a senior, and you stay in the Silver Towers, and you have SUCH a fantastic time."

"WOW!" I said. I was just about to ask what happened if you DIDN'T get five hundred points when the door banged open and four more girls came bursting into the room. When they saw me and Alice they stopped, and stood up straight, and dusted themselves down. The tallest, who was EVER so beautiful in a very pale blonde kind of way, swept us the most amazing curtsey. She went right down to the floor, and she didn't wobble one bit.

"Good afternoon," she said, and her voice was very sweet and clear. "I'm Princess Sophia. These are my friends, the Princesses Katie, Emily and Daisy."

"I'm Alice," Alice said, and she curtsied back – and she didn't wobble either! I felt a tiny bit odd. Every time I tried to curtsey I fell over.

Princess Katie winked at me. She had dancing green eyes, and red-gold hair that curled all over her head.

"Don't be put off by Sophia," she said. "She just can't help showing off. It's a terrible bore for her, being so beautiful, but she's all right really. Who are you?"

"I'm Princess Charlotte," I said. "I've only just got here."

Katie nodded. "Us too," she said, and she sat down on a bed with a most un-princessy flump. "Are you excited about the ball tonight? We are! What are you going to wear? Is your dress here? Can we see it?"

I shook my head. "I've only got my everyday dresses. My ball gowns are coming later, in the luggage cart."

"Mine too," Alice chipped in. "Gran said there wasn't any room in the coach." She giggled. "She and Granpapa came with me, and they both insisted on wearing their coronation robes, and there was only just room for me and the TEENIEST suitcase."

Princess Emily laughed. I'd thought she was a serious kind of girl, but when she laughed her blue eyes twinkled.

"We all came in Sophia's coach...it's ENORMOUS! We rattled about inside like peas in a great big golden pod, but it did mean we could pile loads of luggage on the roof..."

Her voice suddenly trailed away, and she went quite pale.

"What's the matter, Em?" asked Princess Daisy. She was the littlest of us, and she had long black hair, and the biggest brown eyes you ever saw. She patted Emily's hand anxiously. "What's happened?"

"The luggage!" Emily said. "I know the coachman brought in our cases from INSIDE the coach, but I'm almost sure he didn't fetch anything from the OUTSIDE!"

There was a terrible silence.

Then Sophia said, "Are you QUITE sure, Emily?"

Katie dashed to the window, and peered out.

"I can see our cases piled up by the steps," she said.

"And the trunks?" Emily asked, her voice trembling. "Oh, DO say they're there!"

Katie leaned out so far I was scared she'd fall, but she didn't. She pulled herself back in, her eyes shining.

"QUICK!" she said. "The coach is still there – the coachman's talking to the footman by the front door! AND THE TRUNKS ARE ON THE ROOF!"

Chapter Three

We absolutely tore down the stairs, even the elegant Sophia. Surprised heads popped out from doors as we dashed past, but we took no notice. We poured out of the grand front door just in time to see an ancient old coach rumbling away towards the bridge over the river that flowed into the palace lake.

"Our BALL GOWNS!" gasped Sophia.

"Our TIARAS!" wailed Daisy.

Sophia, Emily, Daisy and Katie stared at each other.

"WE'LL HAVE NOTHING TO WEAR FOR THE BIRTHDAY BALL!" Katie said, and the other three burst into floods of tears.

Now, I'm truly not being boastful, but I can run really fast. When I saw how terribly sad Sophia, Katie, Emily and Daisy looked I hitched up my skirts and I SPRINTED after that coach, yelling, "STOP! STOP! PLEASE STOP!!!"

I caught up with it just as it trundled onto the bridge, and I could see the coachman had finally heard me because he turned round to look.

"COME BACK!!!" I shrieked.

I know it wasn't a princessy thing to do, but I HAD to make him stop. At once he pulled hard on the reins, the coach swung wildly – and it was only then I saw the luggage cart lumbering up from the other side...

The CRASH!!!! was terrible. The coach swayed, the cart tipped...and every single trunk and case fell into the river with a humungous SPLASH!!!

I stood and stared. I was so shocked I could hardly breathe.

Alice, Katie, Emily, Daisy and Sophia suddenly appeared beside me, and they stared too. Only bubbles showed where our trunks had landed in the water.

And then an icy cold voice spoke from behind us.

"Princess Charlotte, please come to my study AT ONCE. Princesses Alice, Daisy, Emily, Katie and Sophia, I would like you to go back to your dormitory. NOW!"

Queen Gloriana sounded SO angry my stomach felt as if it was tied into agonising knots.

"Yes, your Majesty," I whispered, and I tried to curtsey – and of course I wobbled so badly I had to clutch at Alice to stop myself falling over.

I wanted to die.

I really really did, especially when Queen Gloriana gave me a totally UTTERLY despising look, turned on her heel, and swept away towards the palace.

Alice slipped her hand into mine. "Oh, Charlotte," she said. "It was an accident."

I began to cry. I couldn't help it. Katie took my other hand.

"We'll come with you," she said.

"We all will," said Sophia. "It was our trunks you were trying to save."

Emily gave me a hankie, and Daisy looked at me solemnly.

"You were very brave," she said. "I could never have run like that."

They were all so kind I felt a little bit better. And when we got to the headmistress's study they insisted on coming in with me. I mumbled my way through a MASSIVE apology, and then Sophia explained about the coach going off, and me trying to stop it, and somehow she made it sound as if I'd almost been a hero...

Queen Gloriana listened without saying a word. She has one of those very calm, regal sort of faces, and although she obviously thought I'd been really REALLY silly she never said so. When Sophia had finished she folded her hands on her desk, and looked hard at me.

"It seems, Charlotte," she said, "that you are fortunate in your friends. And I believe that your heart is in the right place, even if you are too quick to act before you think. By now the luggage will have been rescued from the water, and I have asked the pages to take your ball gowns to Matron's room. If you can persuade Matron, or Fairy G as we call her, to help you, then you may attend this evening's Birthday Ball. If, however, Fairy G decides you are *not* worthy, then you will be excluded, together with your five friends.

In addition you will lose fifty tiara points, which will be a VERY poor beginning to your time here. I feel, Charlotte, that this will teach you a lesson you are unlikely to forget. And now you may go."

We shuffled outside in silence. I can't tell you how awful I felt. It was bad enough to get minus tiara points on my very first day at the Princess Academy, but my other punishment was the worst in the whole wide world.

WE WERE GOING TO MISS THE BIRTHDAY BALL...AND IT WAS ALL MY FAULT!

Chapter Four

As we walked down the corridor we passed a group of princesses looking at a noticeboard. As we got closer they started whispering to each other, and a princess with a long pointy nose said, "THOSE are the girls I was telling you about! They're in BIG trouble! They've got minus tiara points ALREADY!"

And the others sniggered.

Princess Sophia was wonderful. She swept us past with SUCH a superior look on her face I almost giggled.

"Ignore them!" she ordered, in her clear cool voice. "Princesses should support each other at all times, especially when things go wrong!" And she sailed on as if she hadn't a care in the world.

"That was Princess Floreen by the board," Alice said in my ear. "And Princess Perfecta was the one with the snooty stare. She was here last year, but she didn't win enough points to join the

Tiara Club, so she's back here again in the first year with us. My big sis says she's GHASTLY."

"Oh," I said, and then I noticed something. Emily and Daisy were both blowing their noses really really hard, and I instantly knew they were trying not to cry. I made up my mind I HAD to convince Fairy G that my new friends must go to the Birthday Ball, even if I didn't. Maybe – and my stomach felt SO wobbly at the thought – she could give me even MORE minus tiara points instead.

Alice knew the way to the Matron's room, and we soon found ourselves outside a big door with a sign outside that said:

FAIRY GODMOTHER
Matron at the Princess Academy
No frogs, toads or spiders IF you please.
P.S. No headache pills will
be given to dragons.

I took a deep breath, and knocked.

"COME IN!" boomed a loud and echoing voice. I nervously opened the door, and peeped inside.

Fairy G was HUGE. She had an enormous big red face and sticking out hair, and she was dressed in a whole collection of shawls and scarves and floaty drapey things. Behind her a massive log fire crackled and spat, and flames roared away up the chimney.

All around the room were shelves and shelves of bottles and pots and jugs, and strange looking bunches of what might have been herbs. The biggest tabby cat I'd ever seen was curled up on the back of a giant armchair. It was all VERY weird, and a little bit scary.

And then I saw our ball gowns. They were hung over a long rail, and you've NEVER seen anything so terrible. They were covered in weeds and mud, and were dripping all over the carpet. The laces were torn, and the fur was bedraggled...and there was a long loop of dull yellowing stars draped over a heap of torn and tattered petticoats.

Sophia let out a little cry. The others gasped.

Worst of all, Alice let go of my hand and clutched at Katie's arm.

"My BEAUTIFUL dress!" she moaned. "Oh, LOOK at it!"

"SO," Fairy G bellowed, and she was looking straight at me, "YOU'RE THE ONE WHO CAUSED ALL THIS MESS AND

MUDDLE! WHAT HAVE YOU GOT TO SAY FOR YOURSELF?"

I swallowed hard.

"It was SO my fault," I whispered. "I just didn't think. I ran after the coach – and the driver crashed because he was looking back at me…"

And that was the exact moment when a HUGE spark flew out of the fire. It landed on the thick woolly carpet, and the brightest red and yellow flames shot up in the air.

Chapter Five

Everyone screamed. Daisy ran for the door. I could feel my jaw dropping, but I knew what I had to do. I snatched my sopping wet dress from the rail, flung it over the flames, and stamped on it.

There was a nasty smell of burning silk, but the fire was out. I leant against the wall, panting...

...and I saw that Fairy G was LAUGHING!

"Well done, Princess," she said, and her voice was softer now. She turned to the others. "You see, there ARE times when acting fast can save the day. And now Princess Charlotte has saved my carpet, I think she deserves a wish. What would you like, my dear?" And her big red face suddenly looked amazingly friendly.

Of course I wished that Alice, Daisy, Emily, Katie and Sophia could have their dresses back as good as new.

"Excellent," beamed Fairy G, and she snapped her big fat fingers.

Have you ever seen sparkly pink fairy dust? Well, it's LOVELY.

It floats in the air, and smells of strawberries, and gets up your nose in the nicest possible way and makes you sneeze! And when we'd all stopped sneezing, there was the rail full of beautiful beautiful BEAUTIFUL dresses on satin hangers, all looking even better than brand new.

And a row of sparkling tiaras
was balanced on the top.

"OOOOOOOOOOOOOOOH!"
breathed Daisy.

"WOW!" Katie and Emily said
together. "WOW!"

"They're   WONDERFUL!"
sighed Sophia.

Alice tucked her hand into mine.

"Thanks!" she said, and her eyes were starry. "You're a REAL friend."

"Thank you so much, Fairy G!" I said. I was feeling so happy I was practically floating.

And then I saw my own poor, wet, burned black dress still lying in a soggy puddle on the carpet. My stomach did a massive swoop, but I took a deep breath.

After all, it was my own fault. Maybe my lovely new friends would tell me about the Birthday Ball...but I had to fight an enormous lump in my throat before I could speak.

"I'll tidy this away," I said, and I bent to pick the dress up.

Alice was beside me in a flash. "I've got another ball gown," she said. "Please say you'll wear it! PLEASE!"

I looked at Fairy G, a little glimmer of hope flickering inside me. She looked back at me, and stroked her chin thoughtfully.

"Please, Fairy Godmother, please allow Charlotte to go to the ball!" Sophia swept Fairy G one of her fantastic curtseys. Daisy, Emily and Katie curtsied too. "Please," they echoed. "PLEASE!"

Best Friends Forever!

"We wouldn't enjoy it without her," Daisy added. "We're all BEST friends!"

"That's right!" Alice didn't curtsey, but she did a lovely twirl, her tiara held high in the air. "I hereby declare the Rose Room girls best friends FOR EVER!"

I SO wanted to hug Alice when she said that. I'd always been a bit on my own, and I'd been hoping and hoping to find some real friends at the Princess Academy – and now I knew I had! It was still my very first day, and I'd nearly ruined everything – but I was part of something really truly special. And I could see Katie's eyes were shining, and Sophia was smiling, and Emily and Daisy were nodding YES!!! like mad.

Fairy G began to chuckle. "Very well, then," she said. "ALL the members of the Rose Room

shall go to the ball. But I think
Princess Charlotte had better
wear her own dress, don't you?"
And she took my dress from me.

More fairy dust twinkled in the air...and there it was in my arms, and it was SO PERFECT I couldn't believe my eyes. Soft pink, with swirly petticoats just like before...but now it was covered with sparkles of magical fairy dust. It was EXACTLY what I'd always dreamt of.

"Just one more thing," Fairy G said as she opened the door for us. "There'll be no minus points for any of you. In fact–" her eyes began to twinkle "–I'll give each of you twenty PLUS tiara points! Twenty points for true friendship."

We started to thank her, but she waved us away. "Quick quick quick! Some of us have to get ready for the ball!" And she shooed us out...

...and as we went I noticed that her carpet was perfect. Not the teeniest sign of a burn.

Fairy G saw me looking, and she winked as she shut the door firmly behind me.

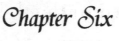

Chapter Six

The Birthday Ball was utterly
GORGEOUS. Did I tell you that
the ceiling of the ballroom was
the most beautiful midnight blue?
And full of twinkling stars? Well,
something AMAZING happened.

All of the new girls were
asked to come in last; Fairy G
said it was a school tradition.

We made sure we Rose Roomers all stayed together, and we were the last to go in...and we were really REALLY nervous. As we swept our way through the golden doors and into the room (would you believe not one of us fell over?) Queen Gloriana was standing by her glittery throne waiting to greet us. We each sank into the deepest curtsey we could manage (even mine was OK!!!) and she smiled, and said, "Welcome to the Princess Academy, my dears."

And then she nodded at Fairy G, who was standing next to her, and Fairy G waved her wand – and SIX NEW STARS popped out of the dark blue sky and shone and shone...and if this sounds boastful I'm really sorry, but OUR STARS WERE THE BIGGEST AND TWINKLIEST OF THEM ALL!!!

Then the music floated us away and round and round in our fabulous ball gowns (would you believe we were ALL wearing pink?) and we danced non-stop until the clock chimed midnight.

It was FABULOUS. And Alice, Daisy, Emily, Katie, Sophia and I chatted and giggled and laughed together all evening, and we had just the very VERY best time...

Fairy G came stomping up the dormitory stairs late that night to check we'd put the light out.

"GOOD NIGHT, ROSE ROOM," she bellowed as she thundered away down the stairs.

And we all snuggled down in our cool white sheets, and I thought how lucky I was to be at the Princess Academy…and I made myself a secret promise. I'd try my VERY best to be a member of the Tiara Club one day, with all my friends…especially you.

The
Tiara
Club

What happens after the
Birthday Ball?

Find out in

and the **Silver Pony**

How do you do? It's LOVELY to
meet you...we're all so glad you're here!
OH! I'm so silly! Maybe you don't know
who we are? We're the Princesses Katie
(that's me), Charlotte, Emily, Alice, Daisy
and Sophia, and we share the Rose Room
Dormitory at the Princess Academy and
one day we'll ALL be members of the
TOTALLY fabulous Tiara Club! Just as long
as we get enough tiara points, of course.
Do you ever feel really TIRED after
a party? Well, we had a WONDERFUL
Birthday Ball here at the Academy,
but for the next few days it
was SO hard to get up...

Check out

website at:

www.tiaraclub.co.uk

You'll find Perfect Princess games and fun things to do, as well as news on the Tiara Club and all your favourite princesses!

Win a Tiara Club
Perfect Princess Prize!

Look for the secret word in mirror writing hidden in a tiara in each of the Tiara Club books. Each book has one word. Put together the six words from books 1 to 6 to make a special Perfect Princess sentence, then send it to us. Each month, we will put the correct entries in a draw and one lucky reader will receive a magical Perfect Princess prize!

Send your Perfect Princess sentence, your name and your address on a postcard to:
THE TIARA CLUB COMPETITION,
Orchard Books, 338 Euston Road,
London, NW1 3BH

Australian readers should write to:
Hachette Children's Books,
Level 17/207 Kent Street, Sydney, NSW 2000.

Only one entry per child.
Final draw: 31 October 2006

The Tiara Club

By Vivian French
Illustrated by Sarah Gibb

PRINCESS CHARLOTTE
AND THE BIRTHDAY BALL   ISBN 1 84362 863 5

PRINCESS KATIE
AND THE SILVER PONY   ISBN 1 84362 860 0

PRINCESS DAISY
AND THE DAZZLING DRAGON   ISBN 1 84362 864 3

PRINCESS ALICE
AND THE MAGICAL MIRROR   ISBN 1 84362 861 9

PRINCESS SOPHIA
AND THE SPARKLING SURPRISE ISBN 1 84362 862 7

PRINCESS EMILY
AND THE BEAUTIFUL FAIRY   ISBN 1 84362 859 7

All priced at £3.99.

The Tiara Club books are available from all good bookshops,
or can be ordered direct from the publisher:
Orchard Books, PO BOX 29, Douglas IM99 1BQ.
Credit card orders please telephone 01624 836000 or fax 01624 837033
or visit our Internet site: www.wattspub.co.uk
or e-mail: bookshop@enterprise.net for details.

To order please quote title, author, ISBN and your full name and address.
Cheques and postal orders should be made payable to 'Bookpost plc.'
Postage and packing is FREE within the UK
(overseas customers should add £2.00 per book).

Prices and availability are subject to change.